Matthew and Emma

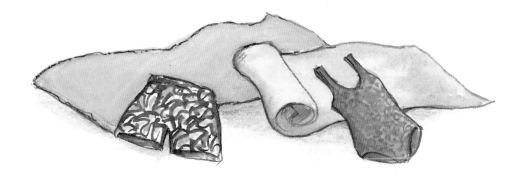

Rigby®

A Harcourt Achieve Imprint

www.Rigby.com
1-800-531-5015

"Look at me," said Matthew.

"I am going down the slide."

"Here I come!"

"Look at me," said Emma.

"Oh no!" said Emma.

"I am **not** going

down the slide."

"Come on, Emma,"

said Matthew.

"Look at me," said Emma.

"I **am** going down the slide."

"Here I come!"